LITTLE RED TRUCK AT THE BEACH

LITTLE RED TRUCK AT THE BEACH

A BOOK FOR KIDS OF ALL AGES

Story by Magic Jack Noel
Illustrated by Magic Jack Noel

XULON PRESS

Xulon Press
2301 Lucien Way #415
Maitland, FL 32751
407.339.4217
www.xulonpress.com

Paperback ISBN-13: 978-1-66282-192-9
Ebook ISBN-13: 978-1-66282-193-6

Inspired in part by a real little
red pickup truck at the beach

Dedicated to my Wife Joan
And
New Covenant Church
Lewes, Delaware

From his window in the big man-sion on the beach, a very rich man could watch the waves crashing on the sand. He had every-thing money could buy. Along with being wealthy he was also well known in the town. In fact, he was chosen to be the Grand Marshall in the town's 4th of July Parade. For this honor he wanted to ride in a gigantic, shiny bright red pickup truck. So a contest was held to pick the best red pickup truck for him to ride down the town's main street during the special parade. Any big new shiny, red pickup truck would feel proud to be the winner of the contest and be in this important parade.

Now, not too far from the beach, in a small cottage, lived a lonely old man. He often walked to the beach early in the morning to watch the sun come up over the crashing waves. He could also walk anywhere he needed to go, like to the board-walk or the store. For bigger trips, he had an ancient – not – too – shinny, little red pickup truck. Some how the little red truck heard about the contest and that the winner would be in the town's big parade. The little red truck thought that if the lonely old man entered him in the contest and won, the rich man would have to pick him to ride in the parade for everyone to see. The little truck really wanted to win this contest. He even prayed about it.

Sure enough the lonely old man entered the little red pickup truck in the contest. Well, the rich man didn't even look at the red – not – so – shiny old truck. Of course a big, new, bright, shiny red truck was the winner. After the contest the lonely old man drove his good old – not – so-shiny little red truck back to the cottage where they lived. Even though the little red truck didn't win, the lonely old man still loved his little red truck. After all, they were always best buddies.

The next day was Sunday. Early in the morning the lonely old man walked to the beach to watch the waves crashing. To his surprise, there was a small group of people setting up something special on the beach not too far from the bandstand. They had lots of equipment to carry to the beach, including a big, heavy wooden cross.

The lonely old man offered to help these nice people and learned that they were setting up to have a church service on the beach. He enjoyed these people so much that he stayed for the service, joined in singing their songs, and really loved the message from the pastor about the real meaning of that heavy wooden cross and about Jesus

After the service, the lonely man offered to use his not – so - shiny red truck to carry the heavy wooden cross back to the church. The red truck was really proud to carry that heavy wooden cross. And then back at the church, the lonely old man met the people who attended the church. They were all so very friendly. So the lonely man got permission from the church pastor to drive that beautiful heavy cross to the beach every Sunday morning in the old – not – so – shiny – little red truck.

By driving to the Church On The Beach every Sunday, the little red truck learned the real meaning of the cross it was carrying. The little red truck was glad he didn't win the parade contest. In fact, he saw that God had a better plan for him. That plan was to carry the big heavy wooden cross to the beach and back to the church every Sunday. God's plan was the best honor in the whole wide world for the little red truck. The little truck was so proud that people said it looked like he had light shining from inside of him. Wow! Now he was brighter than a brand new big red truck. Oh yes, and the lonely old man wasn't lonely at all anymore. He made lots of friends at the church, especially his new very best friend for ever, Jesus Christ.

THE NEW

LITTLE RED TRUCK
AT THE BEACH

CPSIA information can be obtained
at www.ICGtesting.com
Printed in the USA
BVHW020414080921
615480BV00012B/49